© Forlaget Sesam, 2001

Translation: H.P. Paull

Designer: Janus René Andersen

Cover layout: Janus René Andersen

Printer: Nørhaven Book, Viborg

ISBN 87-11-13548-4

1. edition, 4 impression, 200 5

HANS CHRISTIAN ANDERSEN

THE LITTLE
MERMAID

Illustrated by Esben Hanefelt Kristensen

SESAM

Far away, where the ocean is as blue as the prettiest cornflower, and as clear as crystal, it is very, very deep; deeper than the length of any rope: many church steeples, piled one upon another, would not reach from the seabed beneath to the surface above the water. Here resides the Sea King and his subjects.

It is wrong to imagine that nothing exists at the bottom of the sea but bare yellow sand. No, indeed; the most remarkable flowers and plants grow there; the leaves and stems of which are so supple, that the slightest movement of the water causes them to stir as if they had life. Fishes, both large and small, glide between the branches, as birds fly among the trees here upon land. In the very depth of it all, stands the castle of the Sea King. Its walls are built of coral, and the long, gothic windows are of the clearest amber. The shells forming the roof, open and close as the water flows over them. They appear very beautiful, for in each lies a splendid pearl, fit for the diadem of a queen.

The Sea King had been a widower for many years, and his aged mother kept house for him. She was a very wise woman, and exceedingly proud of her high birth; on that account she wore twelve oysters on her tail; while others, also of high rank, were only allowed to wear six. She did, however, deserve great praise, especially for her care of the little sea-princesses, her grand-daughters. They were six beautiful children; and the youngest was the prettiest of them all; her skin was as clear and delicate as a rose-petal, and her eyes as blue as the deepest sea; but, like all the others, she had no feet, and her body ended in a fish's tail.

All day long they played in the great halls of the castle, or among the living flowers that grew out of the walls. The large amber windows were open, and the fish swam in, just as the swallows fly into our houses when we open the windows, only the fishes would swim up to the princesses, eat out of their hands, and allowed themselves to be stroked.

Outside the castle there was a beautiful garden, in which grew bright red and dark blue flowers, and blossoms like flames of fire; the fruit glittered like gold, and the leaves and stems waved to and fro continually. The ground itself was the finest sand, only blue as the flame of burning sulphur. An extraordinary blue lustre surrounded the place, as if it really were situated in the sky above, instead of the dark depths of the sea. In calm weather the sun could be seen, looking like a purple flower, with the light flowing from the calyx.

Each of the young princesses had a little plot of ground in the garden, where she might dig and plant as she pleased. One arranged her flower-bed into the form of a whale; another thought it better to make hers like the figure of a little mermaid; but that of the youngest was round like the sun, and consist of flowers as red as his rays at sunset. She was a strange child, quiet and thoughtful; and while her sisters would be delighted with the wonderful things which they obtained from the wrecks of vessels, she only cared for her pretty red flowers, resembling the sun, and a beautiful marble statue. It was the representation of a handsome boy, carved out of pure white stone, which had fallen to the bottom of the sea from a wreck. She planted by the statue a rose-coloured weeping willow. It grew splendidly, and very soon drooped its fresh branches over the statue, almost down to the blue sands. The shadow had a violet tint, and like the branches, it waved to and fro; as if the crown of the tree and the root were at play, and trying to kiss each other.

Nothing gave her so much pleasure as to hear about the world above the sea. She made her old grandmother tell her all she knew of the ships and of the towns, the people and the animals. Most of all it seemed to her enchantingly beautiful to hear that the flowers of the land should have fragrance, unlike those below the sea; that the trees of the forest should be green; and that the fishes among the trees could sing so sweetly, that it was quite a pleasure to hear them. The grandmother called the little birds fishes, or she would not have understood her; for she had never seen birds.

"When you have reached your fifteenth year," said the grandmother, "you will have permission to rise up out of the sea, to sit on the rocks in the moonlight, while the great ships are sailing by; and then you will see both forests and towns." In the following year, one of the sisters would be fifteen. As each sister was a year younger than the other, the youngest would have to wait five years before her turn came to rise up from the bottom of the ocean, and see the earth as we do. However, each promised to tell the others what she saw on her first visit, and what she thought the most beautiful; for their grandmother could not tell them enough; there were so many things they wanted to know.

The youngest longed more than the rest for her turn to come, she who had the longest time to wait, and who was so quiet and thoughtful. Many nights she stood by the open window, looking up through the dark blue water, and watching the fish as they splashed about with their fins and tails. She could see the moon and stars shining faintly; and through the water they looked larger than they do to our eyes. Then something like a black cloud passed between her and

them, she knew that it was either a whale swimming over her head, or a ship full of human beings, who never imagined that a pretty little mermaid was standing beneath them, reaching out her white hands towards the keel of their ship.

As soon as the eldest was fifteen, she was allowed to rise to the surface of the ocean. When she came back, she had hundreds of things to talk about; but the most beautiful, she said, was to lie in the moonlight, on a sandbank, in the quiet sea, near the coast, and to gaze upon a large town nearby, where the lights were twinkling like hundreds of stars; to listen to the sounds of the music, the noise of carriages, and the voices of human beings, and then to hear the merry bells ringing out from the church steeples; and because she could not go near to all those wonderful things, she longed for them more than ever.

Oh, how the youngest sister listened eagerly to all the accounts, and afterwards, when she stood at the open window looking up through the dark blue water, she thought of the great city, with all its bustle and noise, and even fancied she could hear the sound of the church bells, down in the depths of the sea.

In another year the second sister received permission to rise to the surface of the water,

and to swim about where she pleased. She rose just as the sun was setting, and this, she said, was the most beautiful sight of all. The whole sky looked like gold, while violet and rose-coloured clouds, which she could not describe, floated over her; and, still more rapidly than the clouds, flew a large flock of wild swans towards the setting sun, looking like a long white veil across the sea. She also swam towards the sun; but it sunk into the waves, and the rosy tints faded from the clouds and the sea.

The third sister's turn followed; she was the boldest of them all, and she swam up a broad river that emptied itself into the sea. On the banks she saw green hills covered with beautiful vines; palaces and castles peeped out between the proud trees of the forest; she heard the birds singing, and the rays of the sun were so powerful that she was often obliged to dive down under the water to cool her burning face. In a narrow creek she found a group of little human children, quite naked fooling about in the water; she wanted to play with them, but they fled in fear; then a little black animal appeared; it was a dog, but she did not know that, for she had never before seen one. This animal barked at her so terribly that she became frightened, and rushed back to the open sea. But she said she should never forget the beautiful forest, the green hills, and the lovely little children who could swim in the water, although they did not have fish tails.

The fourth sister was more timid; she remained in the midst of the sea, but she said it was just as beautiful there as nearer the land. She could see for so many miles around her, and the sky above looked like a dome of glass. She had seen the ships, but at such a great distance that they looked like sea-gulls. The dolphins frolicked in the waves, and the great whales spouted water from their blow holes till it seemed as if she were surrounded by a hundred fountains.

The fifth sister's birthday was in the winter; so when her turn came, she saw what the others had not seen the first time they went up. The sea looked quite green, and large icebergs were floating about, each like a pearl, she said, but far greater than the churches built by men. They were of the most wondrous shapes, glittering like diamonds. She had seated herself upon one of the largest, and let the wind play with her long hair, and she noticed that all the ships sailed by rapidly, and steered as far away as they could from the iceberg, as if they were afraid of it. Towards evening, as the sun went down, dark clouds covered the sky, the thunder rolled and the lightning flashed, and the red light glowed on the icebergs as they rocked and tossed on the heaving sea. On all the ships the sails were reefed in alarm and fear, while she sat calmly on the floating iceberg, watching the blue lightning, as it darted its forked flashes into the sea.

Once the sisters had been permitted to rise to the surface, they were each delighted with the new and beautiful sights they saw. And now, being grown-up girls, and able to go when they pleased, they only seemed to lose interest. They wished themselves back again in the water, and after a month had passed they said it was much more beautiful down below, and nice to be at home.

Yet often, in the evening hours, the five sisters would join hands, and rise to the surface. Their voices were more beautiful than any human being's; and before the approach of a storm, when they expected a ship would be lost, they swam before the vessel, and sang sweetly of the delights to be found in the depths of the sea, begging the sailors not to fear if they sank to the bottom. But the sailors could not understand the song, they mistook it for the howling of the storm. These things were never to be beautiful to them; for if the ship sank, the men were drowned, and only their dead bodies reached the palace of the Sea King.

When the sisters would rise, arm-in-arm, through the water, their youngest sister stood all alone, watching them, about to cry, only mermaids have no tears, and therefore suffer more.

"Oh, were I but fifteen years old," said she, "I know that I shall love the world up there, and all the people who live in it."

At last she reached her fifteenth year.

"Well, now, you are grown up," said the old dowager, her grandmother; "so you must let me adorn you like your other sisters;" and she placed a wreath of white lilies in her hair, and every petal was half a pearl. Then the old lady ordered eight great oysters to attach themselves to the princess' tail demonstrating her high rank.

"But they hurt me so," said the little mermaid.

"Pride must suffer pain," replied the old lady.

Oh, how gladly she would have shaken off all this grandeur, and laid aside the heavy wreath! The red flowers in her own garden would have suited her much better, but she did not have the courage to oppose. So she said, "farewell," and rose as lightly as a bubble to the surface of the water.

The sun had just set as she raised her head above the waves; the clouds were tinted with crimson and gold, and through the glimmering twilight beamed the evening star in all its beauty. The sea was calm, and the air mild and fresh. A large ship, with three masts, lay still on the water, with only one sail set; not a breeze stirred, and the sailors sat idle on deck or amongst the rigging. There was music and song on board; and, as darkness fell, a hundred coloured lanterns were lit, as if the flags of all nations waved in the air. The little mermaid swam close to the cabin windows; and now and then, as the waves lifted her up, she could peak through clear glass window-panes, and see a number of well-dressed people within. Among them was a young prince, the most beautiful of all, with large black eyes; he was sixteen years of age, his birthday was being celebrated with much excitement. The sailors were dancing on deck, and when the prince came out of the cabin, more than a hundred rockets rose into the air, turning it

as bright as day. The little mermaid was so startled that she dived under water; and when she again reared her head, it appeared as if all the stars of heaven were falling around her, she had never seen such fireworks before. Great suns spurted fire about, splendid fireflies flew into the blue air, and everything was reflected in the clear, calm sea beneath. The ship itself was so brightly illuminated that all the people, and even the smallest rope, could be seen distinctly. And how handsome the young prince looked, as he shook the hands of all present and smiled at them, while the music sounded in the clear night air.

It was very late; yet the little mermaid could not take her eyes off the ship, or the beautiful prince. The coloured lanterns had been extinguished no more rockets rose in the air, and the cannon had ceased firing. The sea became restless, and a moaning, grumbling sound could be heard beneath the waves: still the little mermaid remained by the cabin window, bobbing up and down on the water, enabling her to look in. After a while, the sails were quickly unfurled, and the noble ship continued her journey; but soon the waves rose higher, heavy clouds darkened the sky, and lightning appeared in the distance. A dreadful storm was approaching; once more the sails were reefed, and the great ship pursued her flying course over the raging sea. The waves grew as high as mountains, as if they wanted to overtop the mast; but the ship dived like a swan between them, and then rose again on their towering, foaming crests. To the little mermaid this appeared pleasant sport; not so to

the sailors. At length the ship groaned and creaked; the thick planks gave way under the lashing of the sea as it crashed down upon the deck; the mainmast snapped in two like a reed; the ship lay over on her side; and water poured in. The little mermaid now understood that the crew were in danger; even she had to be careful to avoid the beams and planks of the wreck, that lay scattered in the water. One moment all was so pitch black that she could not see a single object, then a flash of lightning revealed the whole scene; she could see every member of the ship except the prince. When the ship parted, she had seen him sink into the deep waves, and she was glad, for she thought he would now be with her; and then she remembered that human beings could not live in the water, and when he reached her father's palace he would be quite dead. But he must not die. So she swam about among the beams and planks scattered on the surface of the sea, forgetting that they could crush her to pieces. Then she dived deeply under the dark waters, rising and falling with the waves, till at length she managed to find the young prince, who was fast losing the ability to swim in that stormy sea. His limbs were failing him, his beautiful eyes were closed, and he would have died had the little mermaid not come to his assistance. She held his head above the water, and let the waves carry them where they pleased.

In the morning the storm had ceased; but not a single fragment of the ship could be seen. The sun rose up red and glowing from the water, and its beams brought back a healthy colour to the prince's cheeks; but his eyes remained closed. The mermaid kissed his high, smooth forehead, and stroked back his wet hair; he seemed to her like the marble statue in her little garden, and she kissed him again, wishing that he might live.

Presently they came in sight of land; she saw tall blue mountains, on which the white snow rested as if a flock of swans were lying upon them. Near the coast were beautiful green forests, and close by stood a large building, she could not tell if it was a church or a convent. Orange and lemon trees grew in the garden, and before the door stood noble palms. The sea here formed a little bay, in which the water was quite still, but very deep; so she swam with the handsome prince to the beach, which was covered with fine, white sand, and there she laid him in the warm sunshine, taking care to raise his head higher than his body.

Then bells sounded in the large white building, and a number of young girls came into the garden. The little mermaid swam

from the shore and placed herself between some high rocks that rose out of the water; then she covered her head and neck with the foam of the sea so that her little face might not be seen, as she watched to see what would become of the poor prince.

She did not wait long before she saw a young girl approach the spot where he lay. She seemed frightened at first, but only for a moment; then she fetched a number of people, and the mermaid saw that the prince came to life again, and smiled at those who stood round him. But to her he sent no smile; he did not know that she had saved him. This made her very unhappy, and when he was led away into the great building, she dived sorrowfully down into the water, and returned to her father's palace.

She had always been silent and thoughtful, now more so than ever. Her sisters asked her what she had seen during her first visit to the surface of the water; but she would tell them nothing.

Many an evening and morning did she rise to the place where she had left the prince. She saw the fruits in the garden ripen till they were gathered, the snow on the tops of the mountains melt away; but she never saw the prince, and therefore she returned

home, each time more sorrowful than before. Her only comfort was to sit in her own little garden, and fling her arm round the beautiful marble statue which was like the prince. She gave up tending her flowers, and they grew in wild confusion over the paths, twining their long leaves and stems round the branches of the trees, so that the whole place became dark and gloomy.

Finally she could not bear it any longer, and told one of her sisters all about it. Then the others heard the secret, and very soon it became known to two mermaids whose close friend happened to know who the prince was. She had also seen the celebration on board ship, and she told them where the prince came from, and where to find his palace.

"Come, little sister," said the other princesses; then they joint hands and rose up in a long row to the surface of the water, close to the spot where they knew the prince's palace stood.

It was built of bright yellow shining stone, with long flights of marble steps, one of which reached nearly down to the sea. Splendid gilded domes rose over the roof, and between the pillars that surrounded the whole building stood life-like statues of

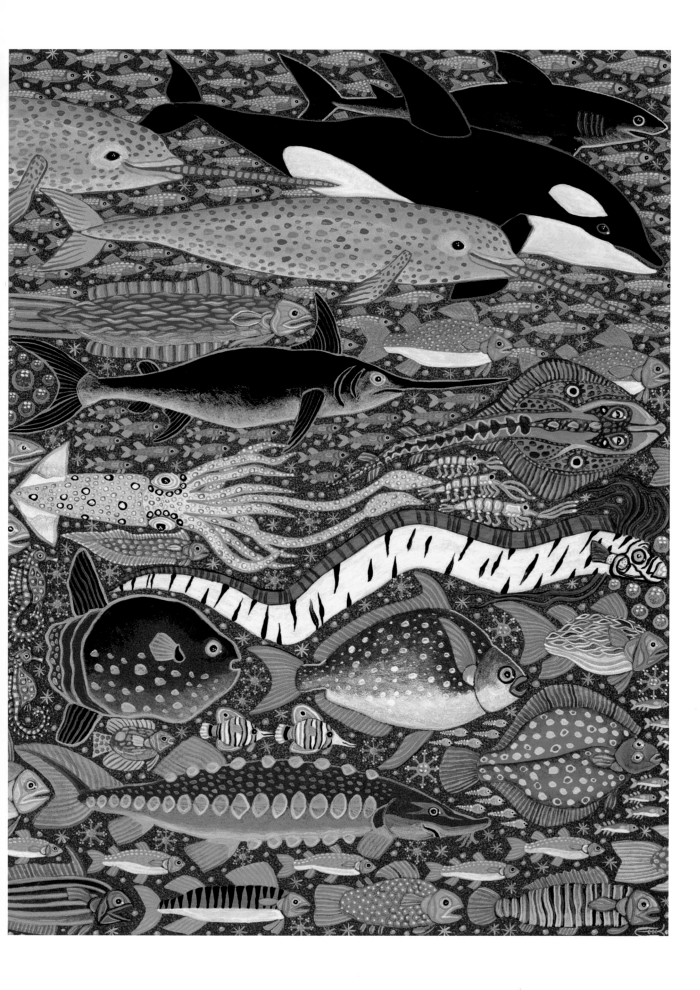

marble. Through the clear crystal of the tall windows could be seen noble rooms, with costly silk curtains and hangings of tapestry; and the walls were covered with beautiful paintings, which were pleasing to look at. In the centre of the largest saloon a fountain spurting its sparkling jets high up into the glass dome of the ceiling. The sun shone down through the dome upon the water and the beautiful plants growing round the basin of the fountain.

Now that she knew where he lived, she spent many an evening and many a night in the sea near the palace. She would swim much nearer the shore than any of the others ventured to do; indeed once she went quite up the narrow channel under the marble balcony, which threw an immense shadow on the water. Here she would sit, watching the young prince, who thought himself all alone in the bright moonlight.

She saw him many times of an evening sailing in a pleasant boat, with music playing and flags waving. She peeped out from among the green rushes, and if the wind caught her long silvery-white veil, those who saw it believed it to be a swan, spreading out its wings.

On many a night, too, when the fishermen, with their torches, were out at sea, she heard them relate so many good things about the doings of the young prince, that she was glad she had saved his life when he had been tossed about half-dead on the waves. And she remembered that his head had rested on her bosom, and how warmly she had kissed him; but he knew nothing of this, and could not even dream of her.

She grew more and more fond of human beings, and wished more and more to be able to wander about with them in their world which seemed to be so much larger than her own. They could fly over the sea in ships, and mount the high hills which were far above the clouds; and the lands they possessed, their woods and their fields, stretched far away beyond the reach of her sight. There was so much that she wanted to know, and her sisters were unable to answer all her questions. Then she implored her old grandmother, who knew all about the upper world, which she very rightly called the lands above the sea.

"If human beings are not drowned," asked the little mermaid, "can they live forever? do they never die as we do here in the sea?"

"Yes," replied the old lady, "they must also die, and their term of life is even shorter than ours. We sometimes live to three hundred years, but when we cease to exist here we merely become foam on the surface of the water, down here we have not even a grave of those we love. We do not have immortal souls, we shall never live again; but, like the green seaweed, when once it has been cut off, we can never flourish again. Human beings, on the contrary, have a soul, which lives forever, lives after the body has turned to dust. It rises up through the clear, pure air beyond the glittering stars. As we rise out of the water, and behold all the land of the earth, they do rise to unknown and glorious regions which we shall never see."

"Why do we not have an immortal soul?" asked the little mermaid mournfully; "I

would give gladly all the hundreds of years that I have to live, to be a human being only for one day. To have the hope of knowing the happiness of that glorious world above the stars."

"You must not think of that," said the old lady; "we feel ourselves to be much happier and much better off than human beings."

"So I shall die," said the little mermaid, "and as the foam of the sea I shall be driven about never again to hear the music of the waves, or to see the pretty flowers nor the red sun. Is there anything I can do to win an immortal soul?"

"No," said the old lady, "unless a man were to love you so much that you were more to him than his father or mother. If all his thoughts and all his love were fixed upon you and the priest placed his right hand in yours, and he promised to be true to you here and hereafter. Then his soul would glide into your body and you would obtain a share in the future happiness of mankind. He would give a soul to you and retain his own as well; but this can never happen. Your fish tail, which amongst us is considered so beautiful, is thought on earth to be quite ugly; they do not know any better, and they think it necessary to have two stout supports, which they call legs, in order to be handsome."

Then the little mermaid sighed, and looked dismally at her fish tail.

"Let us be happy," said the old lady, "and dart and spring about during the three hundred years that we have to live, which is really quite long enough; after that we can go to rest, contended. This evening we are going to have a royal ball."

It is one of those splendid sights, which we can never see on earth. The walls and the ceiling of the large ballroom were of thick, but transparent crystal. May hundreds of colossal shells, some of a deep red, others of a grass green, stood on each side in rows, with blue fire in them, which lighted up the whole saloon, and shone through the walls, so that the sea was also illuminated. Innumerable fishes, great and small, swam past the crystal walls; on some of them the scales glowed with a purple brilliancy, and on others they shone like silver and gold. Through the halls flowed a broad stream, and in it danced the mermen and the mermaids to the music of their own sweet singing. No one on earth has such lovely voices as they. The little mermaid sang more sweetly than the rest. The whole court applauded her with hands and tails; and for a moment her heart felt quite joyful, for she knew she had the loveliest voice of any on earth or in the sea. But she soon thought again of the world above her, for she could not forget the charming prince, nor her sorrow that she had not an immortal soul like his. Therefore she crept away silently out of her father's palace, and while everything within was gladness and song, she sat in her own little garden sorrowful and alone. Then she heard the bugle sounding through the water, and thought, "it is certainly him sailing above, he holds my every wish, in his hands I should like to place the happiness of my life. I will venture all for him, and to win an immortal soul, while my sisters dance in my father's palace, I will go to the sea witch, of whom I have always been so much afraid, but she can give me counsel and help."

And then the little mermaid went out from her garden, and took the road to the foaming whirlpools, behind which the sorceress lived. She had never been that way before: neither flowers nor grass grew there; nothing but bare, grey, sandy ground stretched out to the whirlpool, where the water, like foaming mill-wheels, whirled round everything that it seized, and cast it into the fathomless deep. Through the midst of these crushing whirlpools the little mermaid was obliged to pass, to reach the dominions of the sea witch; and also for a long distance the only road lay right across a quantity of warm, bubbling mire, the witch called her marshes. Beyond this stood her house, in the centre of a strange forest, in which all the trees and flowers were polypi, half animals and half plants; they looked like serpents with a hundred heads growing out of the ground. The branches were long slimy arms, with fingers like flexible worms, moving limb after limb from the root to the top. All that could be reached in the sea they seized upon, and held fast, so that it never escaped from their clutches. The little mermaid was so alarmed at what she saw, that she stood still, and her heart beat with fear, and she very nearly turned back; but she thought of the prince, and of the human soul she longed for, and her courage returned. She fastened her long flowing hair round her head, so that the polypi couldn't seize hold of it. She folded her arms across her bosom, and then she darted forward as fish shoots through the water, between the supple arms and fingers of the ugly polypi, which were stretched out on each side of her. She saw that each held in its grasp something it had seized with its numerous little arms, as if they were iron bands. The white skeletons of human beings perished at sea, and had sunk down into the deep waters, skeletons of land animals, oars, rudders, and chests of ships were lying tightly grasped by their clinging arms; even a little mermaid, whom they had caught and strangled. This seemed the most shocking of all to the little princess.

She now came to a space of bogy ground in the wood, where large, fat water-snakes were rolling in the mire, and showing their ugly, drab-coloured bodies. In the midst of this spot stood a house, built with the bones of shipwrecked human beings. There sat the sea witch, allowing a toad to eat from her mouth, just as people sometimes feed a canary with a piece of sugar. She called the ugly water-snakes her little chickens, and allowed them to crawl all over her bosom.

"I know what you want," said the sea witch; "it is very stupid of you, but you shall have your way, and it will bring you to sorrow, my pretty princess. You want to get rid of your fish tail, and to have two supports instead of it, like human beings on earth, so that the young prince may fall in love with you, and that you may have an immortal soul." And then the witch laughed so loudly

and horribly, that the toad and the snakes fell to the ground, and lay there wriggling about. "You are just in time," said the witch, "for after sunrise tomorrow I should not be able to help you until the end of another year. I will prepare a draught for you, with which you must swim to land tomorrow before sunrise, and sit down on the shore and drink it. Your tail will then disappear, and shrink up into what mankind calls legs, and you will feel great pain, as if a sword were passing through you. But all that see you, will say that you are the prettiest little human being they ever saw. You will still have

the same floating gracefulness of movement, and no dancer will ever tread so lightly; but at every step you take it will feel as if you were treading upon sharp knives, and blood must flow. If you will bear all this, I will help you."

"Yes, I will," said the little princess in a trembling voice, as she thought of the prince and the immortal soul.

"But think again," said the witch, "for when once your shape has become like a human being, you can no more be a mermaid. You will never return through the water to your sisters, or to your father's palace again. If you do not win the love of the prince, so that he is willing to forget his father and mother for your sake, and to love you with his whole soul, and allow the priest to join your hands that you may be man and wife, then you will never have an immortal soul. The first morning after he marries another your heart will break, and you will become foam on the crest of the waves."

"I will do it," said the little mermaid, turning pale as death.

"But I must be paid also," said the witch, "and it is not a trifle that I ask. You have the sweetest voice of any that dwell here in the depths of the sea. You believe that you will be able to charm the prince with it also, but this voice you must give to me; the best thing you possess will I have for the price of my draught. My own blood must be mixed with it, that it may be as sharp as a two-edged sword."

"But if you take away my voice," said the little mermaid, "what is left for me?"

"Your beautiful form, your graceful walk,

and your expressive eyes; surely with these you can enchain a man's heart. Well, have you lost your courage? Poke out your little tongue that I may cut it off as my payment; then you shall have the powerful draught."

"It shall be done," said the little mermaid. Then the witch placed her cauldron on the fire, to prepare the magic draught. "Cleanliness is a good thing," said she, scouring the vessel with snakes, which she had tied together in a large knot; then she pricked herself in the breast, and let the black blood drop into it. The steam that rose formed such horrible shapes that no one could look at them without fear. Every moment the witch threw something else into the cauldron, and when it began to boil, it sounded like the weeping of a crocodile. When at last the magic draught was ready, it looked like the clearest water.

"This is for you," said the witch. Then she cut off the mermaid's tongue, so that she became dumb, and would never speak or sing again.

"If the polypi should seize hold of you as you return through the wood," said the witch, "throw over them a few drops of the potion, and their fingers will be torn into a thousand pieces." But the little mermaid had no need to do this, for the polypi sprang back in terror when they caught sight of the glittering draught, which shone in her hand like a twinkling star. So she passed quickly through the wood and the marsh, and between the rushing whirlpools.

She saw that in her father's palace the torches in the ballroom were extinguished and all within asleep; but she did not venture to go in to them, for now she was dumb and going to leave them forever, she felt as if her heart would break. She crept into the garden, took a flower from the flowerbeds of each of her sisters, kissed her hand a thousand times towards the palace, and then rose up through the dark blue waters.

The sun had not yet risen when she came in sight of the prince's palace, and approached the beautiful marble steps, but the moon shone clear and bright. Then the little mermaid drank the magic draught, and it seemed as if a two-edged sword went through her delicate body: she fainted, and lay as still as the dead. When the sun arose and shone over the sea, she recovered, and felt a sharp pain; but just before her stood the handsome young prince. He fixed his jet-black eyes upon her so earnestly that she cast down her own. Then she became aware that her fish tail was gone, and that she had as pretty a pair of white legs and tiny feet as any little maiden could have; but she had no clothes, so she wrapped herself in her long, thick hair. The prince asked her who she was, and where she came from. She looked at him with gentle and sad deep blue eyes; but she could not speak. Every step she took was as the witch said it would be. She felt as if she were treading upon the points of needles or sharp knives; but she bore it willingly, and stepped as lightly by the prince's side as a bubble, so that he and all that saw her wondered at her graceful-swaying movements.

She was very soon dressed in costly robes

of silk and muslin, and was the most beautiful creature in the palace; but she was dumb, and could neither speak nor sing.

Beautiful female slaves, dressed in silk and gold, stepped forward and sang before the prince and his royal parents: one sang better than all the others, and the prince clapped his hands and smiled at her. This saddened the little mermaid; she knew how much more sweetly she once could sing, and she thought, "oh if only he knew! I have given away my voice forever, to be with him."

The slaves next performed some pretty fairy-like dances, to the sound of beautiful music. Then the little mermaid raised her lovely white arms, stood on the tips of her toes, and glided over the floor, and danced as no one yet had been able to dance. Each moment her beauty became more revealed, and her expressive eyes appealed more directly to the heart than the songs of the slaves.

Every one was enchanted, especially the prince, who called her his little waif; she danced again quite readily, to please him, though each time her foot touched the floor it seemed as if she was stepping on sharp knives. The prince said she should remain with him always, and she received permission to sleep at his door, on a velvet cushion.

He had a page's dress made for her, that she might accompany him on horseback. They rode together through the sweet-scented woods, where the green boughs touched their shoulders, and the little birds sang among the fresh leaves. She climbed with the prince to the tops of high mountains; and although her tender feet bled so that even her steps were marked, she only laughed, and followed him till they could see the clouds beneath them like a flock of birds travelling to distant lands.

At the prince's palace, and when all the household were asleep, she would go and sit on the broad marble steps; for it eased her burning feet to bathe them in the cold sea-water; and then she thought of all those down below in the ocean.

Once during the night her sisters came up arm-in-arm, singing sadly, as they floated on the water. She beckoned to them. They recognized her, and told her how she had grieved them. After that, they came to the same place every night; and once she saw in the distance her old grandmother, who had not been to the surface of the sea for many years, and the old Sea King, her father, with his crown on his head. They stretched out their hands towards her, but they did not venture so near the land as her sisters did.

As the days passed, she loved the prince more fondly, and he loved her as he would love a little child. But it never entered his head to make her his wife; yet, unless he married her, she could not receive an immortal soul; and, on the morning after his marriage to another, she would dissolve into the foam of the sea.

"Do you not love me the best of them all?" the eyes of the little mermaid seemed to say, when he took her in his arms, and kissed her fair forehead.

"Yes, you are dear to me," said the prince, "for you have the best heart, and you are the most devoted to me; you are like a young

maiden whom I once saw, but whom I shall never meet again. I was in a ship that was wrecked, and the waves cast me ashore near a holy temple, where several young maidens performed the service. The youngest of them found me on the shore, and saved my life. I saw her but twice, and she is the only one in the world whom I could love; but you are like her, and you have almost driven her image out of my mind. She belongs to the holy temple, and my good fortune has sent you to me instead of her; and we will never part."

"Ah, he does not know that it was I who saved his life," thought the little mermaid. "I carried him over the sea to the wood where the temple stands: I sat beneath the foam, and watched till the human beings came to help him. I saw the pretty maiden that he loves more than he loves me;" and the mermaid sighed deeply, but she could not shed tears. "He says the maiden belongs to the holy temple, therefore she will never return to the world. They will not meet again. I am by his side, and see him every day. I will take care of him, and love him, and give up my life for his sake."

Very soon a fine ship was being fitted out as it was said that the prince must marry, and that the beautiful daughter of a neighbouring king would be his wife. Although the prince gave out that he merely intended to pay a visit to the king, it was generally supposed that he really went to see his daughter. An immense company were to go

with him. The little mermaid smiled, and shook her head. She knew the prince's thoughts better than anyone else did. "I must travel," he had said to her, "I must see this beautiful princess; my parents desire it; but they will not make me bring her home as my bride. I cannot love her; she is not like the beautiful maiden in the temple, whom you resemble. If I were forced to choose a bride, I would rather choose you, my dumb waif, with those expressive eyes." And then he kissed her rosy mouth, played with her long waving hair, and laid his head close to her heart, while she dreamed of human happiness and an immortal soul.

"You are not afraid of the sea, my dumb child," said he, as they stood on the deck of the noble ship, which was to carry them to the country of the neighbouring king. And then he told her of storm and of calm, of strange fishes in the deep beneath them, and of what the divers had seen there. She smiled at his descriptions, for she knew better than any one what wonders were to be found at the bottom of the sea.

In the moonlight, when all on board were asleep, except the man at the helm, who was steering, she sat on the deck, gazing down through the clear water. She thought she could distinguish her father's palace, and upon it her aged grandmother, with the silver crown on her head, looking through the surge of water at the keel of the vessel. Then her sisters came up on the waves, and gazed at her mournfully, wringing their white hands. She beckoned to them, and smiled, wanting to tell them how happy and well off she was; but the cabin boy approached,

and when her sisters dived down he thought all he was seeing was the foam of the sea.

The next morning the ship sailed into the harbour of a beautiful town belonging to the king whom the prince was going to visit. The church bells were ringing, and from the high towers sounded a flourish of trumpets; and soldiers, with flying colours and glittering bayonets, lined the rocks through which they passed. Every day was a celebration; balls and entertainment followed one another. But the princess had not yet appeared. People said that she was being brought up and educated in a religious house, where she was learning every royal virtue. At last she came.

Then the little mermaid, who was very anxious to see whether she was really beautiful, was obliged to acknowledge that she had never seen a more perfect vision of beauty. Her skin was delicately fair, and beneath her long dark eyelashes her laughing blue eyes shone with truth and purity.

"It was you," said the prince, "who saved my life when I lay dead on the beach," and he held his blushing bride in his arms. "Oh, I am too happy," said he to the little mermaid; "my highest hopes are all fulfilled. You will rejoice at my happiness; for your devotion to me is great and sincere." The little mermaid kissed his hand, and felt as if her heart was already broken. His wedding morning would bring death to her, and she would turn into the foam of the sea.

Every church bell rang out and the heralds rode about the town proclaiming the engagement. Perfumed oil was burning in costly silver lamps on every altar. The priests waved the censers, while the bride and bridegroom joined their hands and received the blessing of the bishop. The little mermaid, dressed in silk and gold, held up the bride's train. But her ears heard nothing of the festive music, and her eyes did not see the holy ceremony; she thought of the night of death ahead of her, and of all she had lost in the world.

On the same evening the bride and bridegroom went on board ship. Cannons were roaring, flags waving, and in the centre of the ship a costly tent of purple and gold had been erected. It contained elegant couches, for the reception of the bridal pair during the night.

The ship, with swelling sails and a favourable wind, glided away smoothly and lightly over the calm sea.

When it grew dark a number of coloured lamps were lit, and the sailors danced merrily on the deck. The little mermaid could not help thinking of her first rising out of the sea, when she had seen similar festivities and joys; and she joined in the dance, poised herself in the air like a swallow when he pursues his prey, and all present cheered her with wonder. She had never danced so elegantly before. Her tender feet felt as if cut with sharp knives, but she did not mind; a sharper pang had pierced through her heart. She knew this was the last evening she should ever see the prince, for whom she had abandoned her kindred and her home; she had given up her beautiful voice, and suffered unheard-of pain daily for him, while he knew nothing of it. This was the last evening that she would breathe the same

air with him, or gaze at the starry sky and the deep sea; an eternal night, without thought or dream, awaited her: she had no soul and now she could never gain one. All was joy and gayety on board ship till long after midnight, she laughed and danced with the rest, while thoughts of death were in her heart. The prince kissed his beautiful bride, as she played with his raven hair, till they went hand in hand to rest in the splendid tent.

Then all became still on board the ship, only the helmsman stood awake at the helm. The little mermaid leaned her white arms on the edge of the vessel, and looked towards the east for the first blush of morning, for that first ray of dawn that would bring her death. She saw her sisters rising out of the flood: they were as pale as herself; but their long beautiful hair waved no more in the wind, and had been cut off.

"We have given our hair to the witch," said they, "to help you, so that you may not die tonight. She has given us a knife: here it is, see it is very sharp. Before the sun rises you must plunge it into the prince's heart. When the warm blood falls upon your feet they will grow together again, forming into a fish tail, and you will once more become a mermaid, and return to us to live for three hundred years before you die and change into the salty foam of the sea. Hurry, now; he or you must die before sunrise. Our old grandmother moans so for you, that her white hair is falling off from sorrow, as ours fell under the witch's scissors. Kill the prince and come back; hurry: don't you see the first red streaks in the sky? In a few minutes the sun will rise, and you will die." And then they sighed deeply and mournfully, and sank down beneath the waves.

The little mermaid drew back the crimson curtain of the tent, and beheld the fair bride with her head resting on the prince's breast. She bent down and kissed his fair brow, then looked at the sky on which the rosy dawn grew brighter and brighter; then she glanced at the sharp knife, and again fixed her eyes on the prince, who whispered the name of his bride in his dreams. She was in his thoughts, the knife trembled in the hand of the little mermaid: then she flung it far away from her into the waves; the water turned red where it fell, and the drops that spurted up looked like blood. She cast one more long, weakening glance at the prince, and then threw herself from the ship into the sea, and felt her body was dissolving into foam.

The sun rose above the waves, and his warm rays fell on the cold foam of the little mermaid. She did not feel as if she were dying. She saw the bright sun, and all around her floated hundreds of transparent beautiful beings. Through them she could see the white sails of the ship, and the red clouds in the sky; their speech was melodious, but too ethereal to be heard by mortal ears, as they were also unseen by mortal eyes. The little mermaid perceived that she had a body like theirs, and that she continued to rise higher and higher out of the foam.

"Where am I?" asked she, and her voice sounded ethereal, as the voice of those who were with her; no earthly music could imitate it.

"Among the daughters of the air," answered one of them. "A mermaid does not have an immortal soul, nor can she obtain one unless she wins the love of a human being. Her eternal destiny depends on the power of another. The daughters of the air do not possess an immortal soul, but can however, by their good deeds, procure one for themselves. We fly to warm countries, and cool the sultry air that destroys mankind with the pestilence. We carry the perfume of the flowers to spread health and restoration. After we have endeavoured for three hundred years at the best of our abilities, we receive an immortal soul and take part in the happiness of mankind. You, poor little mermaid, have tried with your whole heart to do as we are doing; you have suffered and endured and raised yourself to the spirit-world by your good deeds; and now, by striving for three hundred years in the same way, you may obtain an immortal soul."

The little mermaid lifted her glorified eyes towards the sun, and felt them, for the first time, filling with tears. On the ship, in which she had left the prince, there was activity and noise; she saw him and his beautiful bride searching for her; mournfully they gazed at the pearly foam, as if they knew she had thrown herself into the waves. Unseen she kissed the forehead of the bride, and fanned the prince, and then rose with the other children of the air to a rosy cloud that floated through the ether.

"So for three hundred years we shall float like this," said the little mermaid, "till at last we come into the kingdom of heaven."

"And we may even get there sooner," whispered one of her companions. "Unseen we can enter the houses of men, where there are children, and for every day we find a good child, who is the joy of his parents and deserves their love, our time of probation is shortened. The child does not know, when we fly through the room, that we smile with joy at his good behaviour, for we can count one year less of our three hundred years. But when we see a naughty or a wicked child, we shed tears of sorrow, and for every tear a day is added to our time of trial!"

Edvard Eriksen's statue of The Little Mermaid

One of the main tourist attractions in Denmark is The Little Mermaid. Undoubtably a brilliant work of art. She sits in the water's edge on a rock, body turned towards land, but gazing out to sea, searching for her mermaid sisters. The sculptor has succeeded in combining sorrow and pain with a soft sensuality. The location in the water by Langelinie is fabulous.

The brewer Carl Jacobsen, a great patron of the arts, commissioned Edvard Eriksen in 1910 to create a sculpture of The Little Mermaid. Jacobsen had seen a ballet at The Royal Theatre based on H.C. Andersen's fairy tale, and he felt that the fable was so wonderful it also deserved a sculptural representation. Furthermore he believed that the classical naturalism of Edvard Eriksen would be perfect for the job.

Previously Edvard Eriksen (1876-1959) was famed for several works of art bought by the National Art Museum – the statues "Hope" in 1904 and "The Verdict" in 1906 – additionally he was given the prestigious task of creating three statues ("Sorrow", "Memory" and "Love") for the tomb of King Christian IX and Queen Louise at Roskilde Cathedral.

It is claimed that the royal solo ballerina Ellen Price de Plane posed for Edvard Eriksen. Brewer Jacobsen had seen her dance the title role in the ballet at The Royal Theatre. In actual fact it was the artist's wife, Eline Eriksen, that posed for The Little Mermaid and many of Eriksen's other pieces. Nevertheless Ellen Price did pay several visits to Eriksen's studio, during the process.

In the first draft, the artist chose to portray the mermaid after her transformation into a human being – giving her feet – but after many considerations, and discussions with Carl Jacobsen, her final representation was with a fish tale. In the autumn of 1910 Eriksen finalized the plaster model, and in 1911 court bronze forger, Carl N.G. Rasmussen, crafted the bronze cast.

Not before September 1912 would the Mermaid have a trial showing by Langelinie, also back then this was a popular site for excursions – many townsfolk took their Sunday stroll here. But the statue was situated too low and too near the coast. It would take almost a year to move her position, finally The Little Mermaid was placed in her present setting on August 23rd 1913.

The following years saw the Mermaid's popularity increasing rapidly, on several

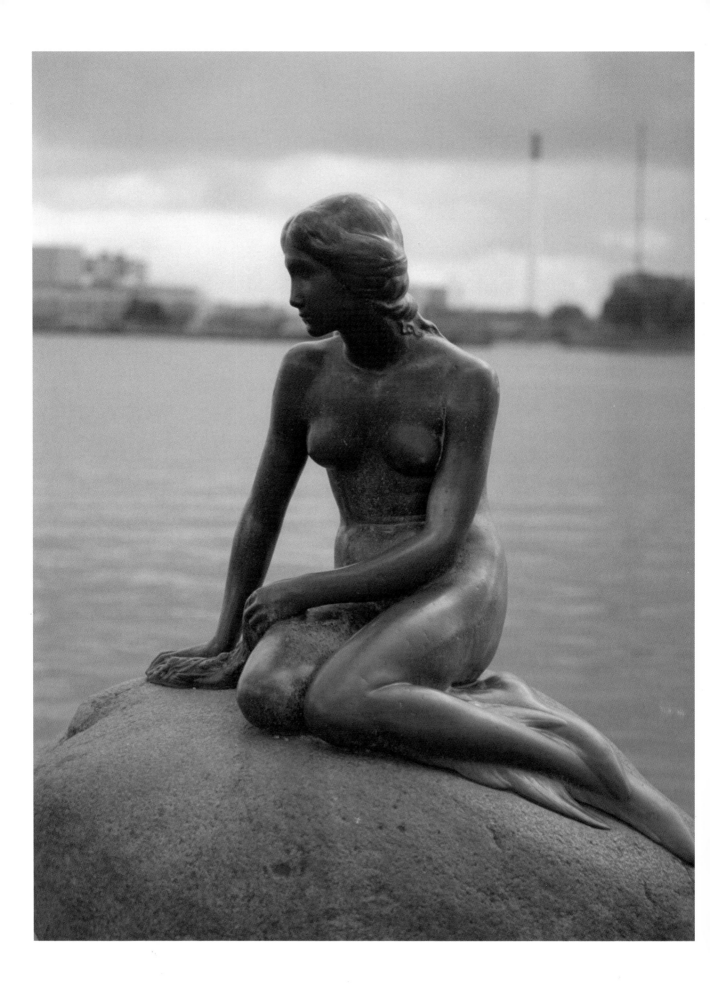

occasions Edvard Eriksen was approached to sell a full size cast of her. He rejected the offers, and it is written in his will that reproductions of the sculpture can only be produced in a smaller scale. In 1995 a bronze copy was made in the scale 4:5, this is to be found in the Japanese port Osaka.

The Little Mermaid has conquered many hearts. She is undoubtably the most photographed woman in Copenhagen, and her 25th, 50th, 75th, and 80th anniversaries have been celebrated with flowers. And like other celebrities she has been under attack – for instance by being covered in paint. In April 1964 the Mermaid's head was severed, creating massive media attention, and resulting in huge worldwide support. The damage was remedied by court bronze forger Poul Lauritz Rasmussen, who created a new head from the original plaster model. So there she sits, sad and dreamy – torn between her feelings for her father and sisters, and her longing for the prince and an immortal soul. And there she stays, every year, seen and admired by visitors from all over the world.